This book
belongs to

_____

_____

For my Normandy neighbours
Victor and Octavie Ferey
F.S.

For Mum
C.J.C.

First published in 1999 in Great Britain by David & Charles Children's Books
Published in this edition in 2005 by
Gullane Children's Books
an imprint of Pinwheel Limited
Winchester House, 259-269 Old Marylebone Road,
London, NW1 5XJ

2 4 6 8 10 9 7 5 3

Text © Francesca Simon 1999
Illustrations © Caroline Jayne Church 1999

A CIP record for this title is available from the British Library.

The right of Francesca Simon and Caroline Jayne Church to be identified
as the author and illustrator of this work has been asserted by them
in accordance with the Copyright, Designs and Patents Act, 1988.

ISBN 1-86233-596-6

Printed and bound in Singapore

HUGO
and the
BULLY FROGS

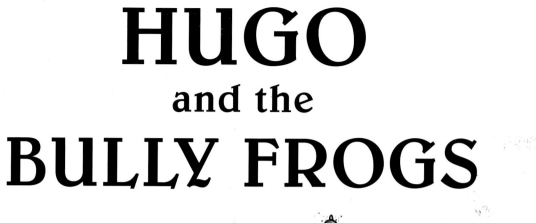

Written by Francesca Simon
Illustrated by Caroline Jayne Church

GULLANE™
CHILDREN'S BOOKS

Once upon a time there lived a very small frog with a very small croak. His name was Hugo. Hugo lived in a deep, muddy pond.

Unfortunately for Hugo, other frogs lived there too.
Big frogs. Mean frogs. Grouchy frogs.
The biggest, meanest and grouchiest frog
of all was Pop Eyes, the leader.

Brr-ack, Brr-ack! We're on the attack!

The big, bad, bullyfrogs swaggered through the reeds
pushing and shoving and showing off, and making
a terrible hullabaloo.

When the bullyfrogs weren't making a hullabaloo,
they liked to sneak up behind Hugo, lift him up,
dangle him upside down and then drop him
in the pond.

Ribbet, Ribbet! Flibbertigibbet!

Croak, Croak! You're a joke!

Hugo hated being pushed. He hated being shoved. Most of all he hated being dropped head first into the pond. But what could he do? He was so little.

He tried being friendly, but it was no use.
If Hugo was playing with a stick, Pop Eyes would snatch it.
If Hugo had a ball, Pop Eyes would kick it away.
If Hugo had a dandelion, Pop Eyes would blow it first.

Pop Eyes made Hugo's life horrid.

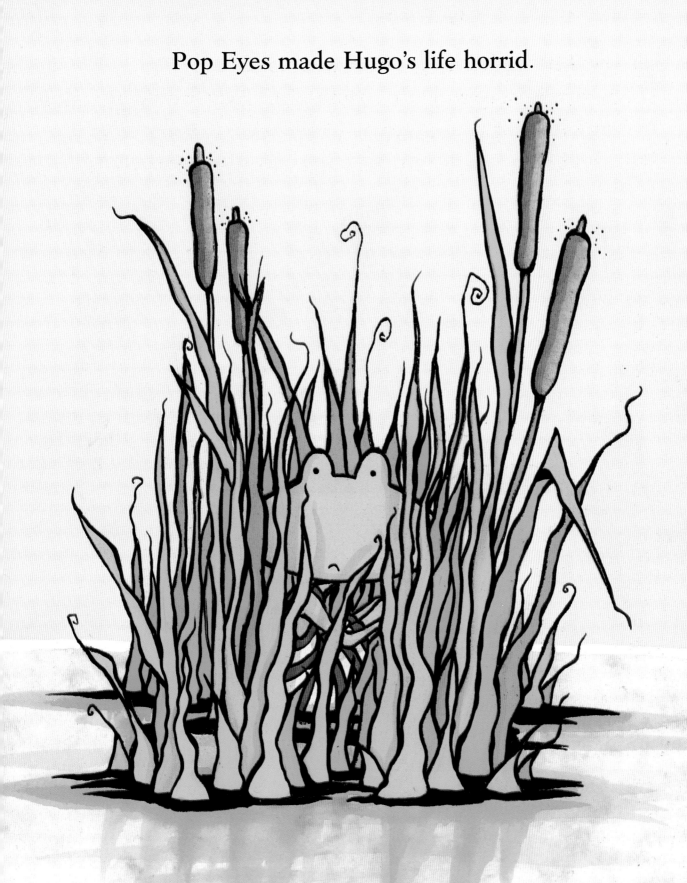

Everyone at the pond offered advice.
"The next time Pop Eyes pushes you,
push him back," said the fish.
"The next time Pop Eyes splashes you,
splash him back," said the dragonfly.
"I can't," said Hugo.

"Why not?" said the duck.

"My head tells my hand to splash, but my hand won't do it," said Hugo sadly.

"Hugo, are you a frog or a fly?" said the duck.

"A fly," squeaked Hugo.

"Nonsense," said the duck.
"We're going to practise. When I push,
you shout, "NO PUSHING!"
The duck butted him with her bill.
"No pushing," whispered Hugo.

"Louder!" said the duck.

"No pushing," murmured Hugo, a little louder.

"I can't hear you," said the duck.

"No pushing!" squeaked Hugo. "It's no use," he said.

"I am a little frog, with a little croak."

The duck thought for a moment.
"You do have a little croak," she said.
"But perhaps you have a loud quack."
"A loud quack?" said Hugo.
"Why not?" said the duck. "Now copy me."
And she quacked, "NO PUSHING!"
in her big, loud, strong, duck voice.

ACK!

"Now you try, Hugo!" said the duck.
Hugo breathed in as much air as he could.
Hugo puffed up his cheeks as fat as he could.
Then he opened his mouth as wide as he could
and bellowed...

QU

ACK!

Birds scattered.
Butterflies fluttered.
Fish flapped.

Then Hugo heard a horrible hullabaloo.
Before he could hop off and hide,
he was surrounded.

"Brr-ack, Brr-ack! We're on the attack!" shrieked Pop Eyes.
"Croak, Croak! You're a joke!" screeched Mudskipper.
"Ribbet, Ribbet! Flibbertigibbet!" rasped Puffy.
"Let's get him, boys!" shouted Pop Eyes.

Birds scattered.
Butterflies fluttered.
Fish flapped.
And the bullyfrogs fell into the pond... **SPLASH!**

Pop Eyes came gasping to the surface.
"How did you do that?" he spluttered.
"Do what?" said Hugo. "Oh do you mean..."

But the bullyfrogs didn't wait around to find out.

Other Gullane Children's Books
for you to enjoy:

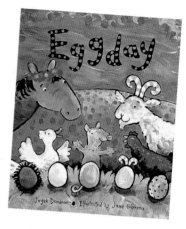

Eggday

JOYCE DUNBAR • JANE CABRERA

Don't Worry, Mouse!

CLAIRE FREEDMAN • SALLY HOBSON

Shoe Shoe Baby

BERNARD LODGE • KATHERINE LODGE

An Itch To Scratch

DAMIAN HARVEY • LYNNE CHAPMAN

GULLANE
CHILDREN'S BOOKS